DINO
PETS
GO TO SCHOOL

Lynn Plourde · illustrated by Gideon Kendall

SCHOLASTIC INC.

ISBN 978-0-545-49560-8

Text copyright © 2011 by Lynn Plourde.
Illustrations copyright © 2011 by Gideon Kendall.
All rights reserved. Published by Scholastic Inc.,
557 Broadway, New York, NY 10012,
by arrangement with Dutton Children's Books,
a division of Penguin Young Readers Group, a member of Penguin Group (USA) Inc.
SCHOLASTIC and associated logos are trademarks and/or registered trademarks of Scholastic Inc.

12 11 10 9 8 7 6 5 4 3 2 1   12 13 14 15 16 17/0

Printed in the U.S.A.   40

First Scholastic printing, September 2012

Designed by Jason Henry

For waggy Maggie,
my favorite pet and chaos creator
—L.P.

·······································

For Milo
—G.K.

Our teacher said,
"It's Pet Day!
So bring your pets
to school to play."

I brought a dino
for a pet,
the **TALLEST** dino
I could get.

When it sat down
on the bus,
the driver made
a great big fuss.

I brought a dino
for a pet,
the **LOUDEST** dino
I could get.

After I made
the introduction,
our whole classroom
needed reconstruction.

I brought a dino
for a pet,
the SPIKIEST dino
I could get.

At recess time
we played a game.
Our soccer ball
was *not* the same.

I brought a dino
for a pet,
the **WIDEST** dino
I could get.

The bench sagged
when it sat for lunch
and food went flying
before we could munch.

I brought a dino
for a pet,
the SMARTEST dino
I could get.

I wanted help
with my math test.
But he ate my quiz . . .

and all the rest.

My teacher gave
the longest sigh,
rolled her eyes,
said, "One more try."

I brought a dino for a pet,
the YOUNGEST dino
I could get.

The teacher thought
this dino was cute,
but the kids said, "Boring!
Can't it hiss or hoot?"

Look who hatched!

HOORAY!

My pets learned
lots at school today.

But school's out . . .

It's time to play!

DINO FACTS

We couldn't actually take dinosaurs to school on Pet Day—they're extinct! But it's fun to imagine dino pets at school. Do you think they'd follow all the rules?

The **TALLEST** dinosaur was *Sauroposeidon* (SORE-oh-po-SIDE-on). When scientists first discovered its neck bones, they'd thought they'd found prehistoric tree trunks. But instead they were four-foot-long hollow neck bones! *Sauroposeidon* was shaped like a giraffe, but it was 60 feet tall.

The **LOUDEST** dinosaur was likely *Parasaurolophus* (pah-ra-sore-OLL-oh-fuss). It had a six-foot-long hollow bone called a crest on top of its head. The *Parasaurolophus* took in air through its nostrils and then made a loud blasting noise with its crest. These dinosaurs moved together in herds and their sounds may have been a way to communicate with other members of their herd.

The **SPIKIEST** dinosaur may have been *Styracosaurus* (STIH-rack-oh-SORE-us) whose name means "spiked lizard." All these spikes may have helped the *Styracosaurus* to protect itself from its predators, but it wouldn't have attacked other dinosaurs since it was an herbivore, or plant-eater.

The **WIDEST** dinosaur was *Ankylosaurus* (ang-KYL-o-sawr-us) which was only four feet tall, but six feet wide. Weighing 10,000 pounds and with short legs, the *Ankylosaurus* would lie flat on the ground to protect itself with hard plates covering most of its body.

The SMARTEST dinosaur may have been *Troodon* (TRUE-oh-don). Scientists believe dinosaur "smarts" can be determined by comparing the size of a dinosaur's brain to the size of its body. Many dinosaurs had huge bodies with tiny brains, but *Troodons* were about the same size as humans, with relatively big brains. Scientists think they would have been as smart as early mammals like opossums or modern-day birds.

The YOUNGEST dinosaur would have been a baby dinosaur! Baby dinosaurs hatched from eggs. Paleontologists have discovered fossils of dinosaur eggs that range in size from one inch up to eighteen inches. Dinosaur eggs were laid in burrows (holes dug in the ground) or nests (sand or mud packed into circular shapes). Some dinosaurs stayed and cared for their eggs while others laid the eggs and then left the young dinosaurs that hatched to fend for themselves.

Keep in mind that dinosaur "facts" may change in the future as other dinosaur bones and fossils are discovered and scientists learn more about these prehistoric creatures. Dinos cannot go to school, but maybe one day *you* will go to school and learn to be a paleontologist (dinosaur scientist). Your research and dinosaur digs and discoveries might lead to new facts about our dino friends.